About this book

Many children have difficulty puzzling out letters because they
are abstract symbols. Letterland's worldwide success is all about its
enduring characters who give these symbols life and stop them from
being abstract. In this book we meet Clever Cat. Her story is carefully
designed to emphasise the sounds that the letter 'C' makes in words.
This definitive, original story book is an instant collector's classic,
making learning fun for a new generation of readers.

A TEMPLAR BOOK

This edition published in the UK in 2008 by Templar Publishing
an imprint of The Templar Company plc,
The Granary, North Street, Dorking, Surrey, RH4 1DN, UK
www.templarco.co.uk

First published by Hamlyn Publishing, 1985
Devised and produced by The Templar Company plc

Copyright © 1985 by The Templar Company plc

1 3 5 7 9 8 6 4 2

ISBN 978-1-84011-765-3

Printed in China

Letterland © was devised by and is the copyright of Lyn Wendon
LETTERLAND® is a registered trademark

Classic LETTERLAND *Storybooks*

Clever Cat and the Clown

Written by Richard Carlisle

Illustrated by
Jane Launchbury

templar publishing

Clever Cat was feeling cosy.
Curled up on a cushion in
the Letterland castle, she fell
asleep and dreamed.

She dreamed of cream cakes.
She dreamed of climbing trees.
The she dreamed that she could
hear curious noises.

Clever Cat woke up. The noises were
still there!
"Wherever are they coming from?"
thought Clever Cat. So she went to
find out.

Outside in the castle courtyard
it was nearly dark.
Clever Cat looked around,
but she could not see anyone.

"That's curious," she thought.
She crept across the courtyard,
waiting for the noise to come again.

It did. It came from behind some
creepers in a corner of the courtyard.
There behind the creepers Clever Cat
found a clown – a clown who was
crying.

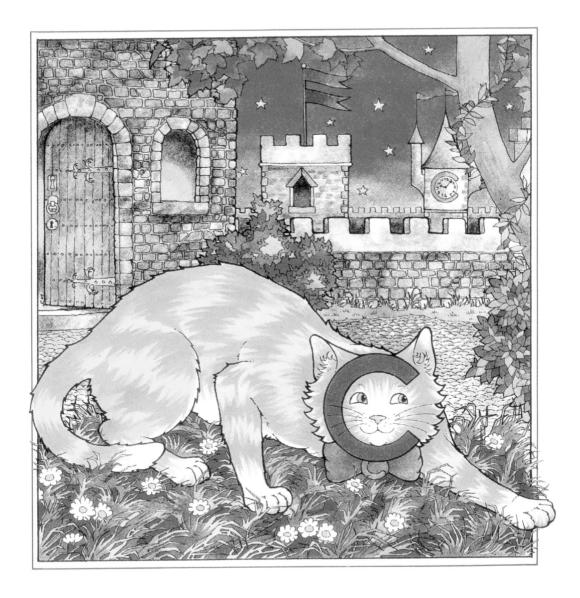

The clown had a tall hat with a crimson bobble on top.
He wore baggy trousers and a baggy shirt with lots of crimson spots on it.

He even had a crimson nose and lips painted red to make people smile at him…

…except that it's hard to smile at a clown who is crying.

Clever Cat looked up at the clown. The clown looked sadly down. A large teardrop slid from the corner of his eye and rolled down his cheek. Another tear splashed on to Clever Cat's head.

Clever Cat did not like getting wet.

"Come along, come along, Mr Clown," said Clever Cat rather crossly, as she wiped the teardrop from her fur. "Tell me what's wrong and I'll try to put it right."

"Oh dear, oh dear," sniffed the clown, "I'm so confused I can't remember where I live. I've lost my memory."

"Crumbs," said Clever Cat, "that's careless. But don't cry. I can usually help. That's why everyone calls me Clever Cat."

"First come into the castle and I'll find you something to eat."

L uckily the castle cook was
nowhere to be seen.
So Clever Cat and the clown
helped themselves to cakes and
ice-cream. That made them both feel
a lot better.

Then Clever Cat started to think hard.
"I wonder where a clown would live?"
she said out loud.

"In a castle?" said the clown hopefully.

"That's silly," said Clever Cat. "What about a cave?"

"Too cold," said the clown. "How about a cottage?"

"Not very likely," said Clever Cat.

"But I must live somewhere," cried the clown. "Everyone lives somewhere."

They thought and thought until morning came. Finally Clever Cat had an idea.

"How about a camp?"

"Maybe..." said the clown.

"Or a caravan?" said Clever Cat.

"That's it!" cried the clown,
jumping off his chair.
"I live in a caravan camp!
Oh how clever you are, Clever Cat.
How very, very clever! I can remember
everything now."

"We were having a clown contest. I am the cannonball clown. So the other clowns shot me over to the castle to invite the King and Queen to come and see our show. But I landed on my head with such a bump that I couldn't remember a thing."

And, sure enough, when they looked over the castle wall, they could see a crowd already collecting around the caravans.

People were arriving from all over Letterland. The sounds of trumpets filled the air. That meant the King and Queen were coming too.

The show was about to begin!

The clown was overjoyed at remembering where he lived, so he cartwheeled all the way to the caravans.

Clever Cat was so pleased with her cleverness that she tried a cartwheel too. But she looked rather clumsy.

"Oh well," she thought. "A cat can't be clever at everything."

THE END